Sea

K. J. Orr was shortlisted for the BBC National Short Story Award in 2011. Her writing has been broadcast on BBC Radio Four, and published by Comma Press, *The Sunday Times Magazine* online, *The White Review*, and *#NewWriting*, among others.

The Inland Sea

K. J. ORR

DAUNT BOOKS

First published in 2012 by
Daunt Books
83 Marylebone High Street
London W1U 4QW

1

Copyright © K. J. Orr 2012

A CIP catalogue record for this title is
available from the British Library.

ISBN 978 1 907970 26 9

Typeset by Antony Gray
Printed and bound by The Aldgate Press

For my mother

ON THE FAR SIDE THE lake is divided from the hills by a slash of soft pink that arrived with the dawn.

They set out, stepping over a yawning crack where the ice has buckled. All along the shore line the lake has twisted, churning the ice into contortions which it has thrown up and aside, forming banks of frozen rubble softened only by fresh snowfall. Ahead of them the ice smoothes out, leaving its fretted edges behind, coursing towards the other side.

They would normally carry their father's bore, or fishing rods, or both, but their hands are empty. Having made their decision they had wrapped themselves up with every layer they could find.

Yet still they are lung-punched, speech-less for now with the cold.

It is so early that the last of the stars are still out. The morning is clear. Pyotr imagines them seen from the hillside up above the village behind – two dark figures against all that white. He had once climbed up there with his father and they had looked out from maybe a thousand metres up, and he had seen the tiny, matchbox houses below and the people, splinter-small. The lake had looked narrow – like a river, like something you could just step across.

He stops and looks back.

He sees the row of wooden houses, the roofs and windows with their splashes of blue paint, their own a straightforward brown. He sees the red iron girders of the railway. He sees the thin line of smoke rising from behind their home where they had left their father standing at the brazier. He would not be watching them.

8

A little way along the shoreline a turquoise boat sits, prow facing the frozen waters, its colour sprung alive against the snow.

Turning, he sees his brother some way ahead of him now, a small figure with a red balaclava moving out across the ice. To the north, which they'll keep on their right hand side as they walk, the lake stretches off, far away beyond, four hundred miles.

When they reach the fishing huts – miniature shelters thrown together from wood and tarpaulin a few hundred feet from the shore – they stop. It is automatic. This is as far as either of them has been on the ice before. In the summer, with their father, they had gone out in the boat much further than this, but never on the ice.

'People drive cars over all of the time,' Pyotr says.

'I know.' Golom plants himself on a wooden crate beside one of the huts. He curls his mittens into imperfect binoculars and surveys the scene from his perch. 'I'm not scared,' he says. 'Are you?'

Pyotr throws him a scornful look. 'It's March.' The ice would be solid for at least another month. It wasn't until May that it started to melt and pull apart. 'Come on,' he says, swivelling his feet around.

They walk in silence keeping up a good pace. Pyotr's eyes are on the thin band of colour that seems to be hovering on the far shore.

His earliest memories are of his father heading off onto the ice, returning hours later, breath steaming, the skin on his face burning with the cold and the exertion. As a child, he would marvel at the chapped skin of his hands, their leathery feel. He remembers him coming in from a snowstorm, clapping both large palms around his own soft hands, and the shock of cold-heat that transferred itself from his father's skin to his own. He remembers watching over and over, from the yard or from the window, as his father disappeared into that limitless expanse; slowly moving, slowly shrinking. His mother, in these memories, is no more than an awareness – the sense of her like a pulse that travels up his spine, keeping his back straight, his eyes sharp. She must have been there then, those times, close by, maybe even at his side, but he finds it hard now to remember her face. It is seven years since she died. They have only one photograph, and in it she doesn't look like herself.

'What have we got to eat?' Golom asks. His cheeks are flushed with the cold and his eyes are streaming, but he has the sleepy stare of still waking up. His breath comes in clouds.

'You'd know if you'd packed the bag,' Pyotr says. 'You'd know if you were the one carrying it.'

'I'm smaller than you.'

'You're stubbier.'

Before being rechristened Golom he was known as Stubby on account of his stockiness and strength. Although he was only small, he had impressed even their father with a natural toughness, an ability to endure physical strains with a degree of joy. He seemed still to surprise himself with this facility, as if he'd just woken up to discover secret powers.

'I can carry the bag too, can't I?' he asks.

'Yes you can,' says Pyotr. 'We'll change over halfway.'

'How will we know when we're half-way?'

'It'll be obvious.' Pyotr waits for his brother to challenge him on this but he doesn't. You never could tell when he would suddenly decide he'd had enough and want the answers to everything.

Last summer a man had come to the lake to do experiments. He was part of an environmental team, and came to their father's yard wanting use of a boat. He spoke Russian – which was why he had been sent ahead of his group to set things up. He knew everything about the lake and what was in it. He was the one who had given Stubby his new name.

Stubby was incredible in the water; not only could he stay in far longer than anyone else without feeling the cold, but somehow he just couldn't float on the surface, and had learned to let himself sink to the bottom and dwell down there like a fish, only now and then coming up for air. The man – Dec-Lan – had

never seen anything like it. He had
wanted to research Stubby's condition
and find out the proper name for it.
They had not known before then that it
was the sort of thing to have its own
name.

Dec-Lan had rechristened Stubby
after the small fish that existed only in
this lake; the golomyanka. Dec-Lan told
Stubby that most people who swam for
long times in cold water had to rub fat
all over their skin. The golomyanka was
35% fat and lived deep down in the
water. Dec-Lan told Stubby he was
more golomyanka than boy.

'It's like you have a wetsuit under
your skin,' he said. 'We'll have to take
you to the lab and have a closer look.'

Stubby had looked wary until Dec-
Lan's face cracked into a smile.

'*You're-all-right*,' Dec-Lan had said,
in English. This was something he
said a good bit, '*You're-all-right*.' Pyotr

couldn't be sure what it meant, but he liked the sound, the way the words came out.

Far ahead of them he can see conifers, and birches – slivers of upright silver lining the banks of the lake. With their father they have been to the forests where the trees are lined up like ghostly battalions, clouding the horizon in layered multitudes, even then barely there. Dead souls, their mother would have said.

Her curiosity towards old superstitions had come laced with a love of ambiguity. Details so familiar they were considered fact would be entirely altered. She would decide for herself, as the mood took her, who was good and who was evil among the lake spirits. You could never tell how a story would end. Pyotr never could decide whether the lake island was home to a demon, and as many times as they had made the trip out there in his father's boat, he had yet to set foot on shore.

The sun is making its slow ascent. The air is empty, noiseless. The sound of their feet alone.

Pyotr stops, closes his eyes.

'What?' Golom asks.

'Stop.'

'What is it?'

'Stop talking.'

'What?'

'Just shut up.'

He hears his brother step closer to him and then stop. They stand beside each other listening. For a moment, there is no sound at all.

'I can't hear anything,' Golom says.

'Exactly.'

'*Jay-sus.*' This was something else Dec-Lan had said.

Smiling, Pyotr opens his eyes and sees snow falling like lazy butterflies. Golom starts leaping, waving his arms around him and clapping his hands together to try to catch the flakes. Pyotr feels the cold drops of moisture landing on his face. 'Stop jumping around,' he says to Golom. 'You'll use all your energy.' Golom stands still and tries instead to catch a snowflake on his tongue. 'Do that too long, your tongue will freeze and drop off.' Golom looks circumspect; he starts flicking his tongue in and out rapidly, like a lizard, or a frog. A moment later he stops.

'When can we eat?'

'When do you want to eat?'

'Now.' He looks defiant. He knows it's too early.

They eat watching the snow fall around them. It seems to be coming out of nowhere. There are wisps of cloud up above, nothing more.

Golom sits with the backpack flat beneath him, his legs stretched out in front. He looks towards home, then to the far bank, and then back again towards home. 'How far have we come?' he asks. He takes another bite of bread. He sits there chewing, swinging his legs open and shut like windscreen wipers on the ice.

Pyotr tries to gauge the distance. 'A few miles,' he says.

'How many exactly?'

'Maybe five?'

'Five?'

'Maybe.'

Golom has stopped moving his legs and is sitting very still now, peering through the ice.

'Anything down there?' Pyotr asks. He remembers when they went out on the water, and Dec-Lan told tales about prehistoric crocodiles lurking just beneath the boat and Golom shivered with delight.

'All we ever have is smoked fish,' Golom says.

*

Beneath them the ice is glistening silver
in the early light. Pyotr always felt that
you should be able to see right through to
the water beneath. Sometimes it looked
so transparent – it seemed to him there
should be something down there waiting
to be seen.

He remembers sitting in the boat with
his father as somewhere beneath them
Dec-Lan swam. He didn't really understand what he got up to down there.
He imagined him sometimes swimming,
sometimes floating, looking about,
bubbles streaming from his mask. When
he reappeared Pyotr found it hard
not to look pleased. Dec-Lan would be
grinning as he flung his arms over the
side and pulled himself up, landing black
and shiny in his wetsuit at their feet.
'*Jay-sus!*'

His father didn't speak to Dec-Lan.
He would guide the boat out onto the

lake until he was asked to stop, and then cut the engine. If they began to drift he would start it up and adjust their position before cutting it again.

Golom lies flat on his back now. 'How much longer will it take?' he says.

'Are you tired?'

'No.'

'Are you sure?'

'Yes.'

'Maybe an hour,' Pyotr says. 'Maybe it'll take an hour.'

His brother starts making duck noises, staring at the sky. He pulls an invisible rifle from his shoulder, aims, fires.

'Have you finished eating?'

'Yes.'

'Do you want some tea?'

'No.'

'Let's go.'

Pyotr watches Golom slowly getting

to his feet and regrets having stopped so early. He feels somehow they have lost momentum, that they should have kept going and eaten as they went.

At the far side the ice is gleaming coolly in the sunlight.

As they set off again he tries to get a sense of the distances involved. He looks towards the southern end of the lake. A landmark would make things easier, but there are only the usual scatterings of houses lining the banks. He needs something like the paper mill that will mark out their home from the other side, when they look back.

He wonders whether he should have brought a map, or a compass, though the thought had not crossed his mind when he packed his bag. He had never seen his father use these things. It was a clear day, conditions were perfect. When people talked about the breadth of the lake they talked about the farthest reaches, where it was forty miles across, not here, where it tapered. The distance was nothing in comparison. When he found out, his father probably wouldn't even be impressed.

Pyotr had spent his childhood familiar with the smells of the boatyard. His father brought home the tar and the varnish, though he would wash in the shower he had rigged outside their home before coming in to eat.

Sometimes Pyotr would lean out of a window to watch as his father snarled under the cold water. 'Over here!' he would yell, and his father would play act some forest creature, straining his arms towards him, gnashing his teeth. When he reappeared, freshly-washed, traces of the yard would still betray him – spots and stains on the skin of his face and forearms.

One morning late last summer, he had caught Pyotr by the sleeve, brought him to the yard, and planted him on the smooth, warm hull of an overturned boat. 'Watch,' was all he had said. Pyotr had tried to watch, though he couldn't see the point, not knowing what it was that he was watching. Men moved around the yard, stopping occasionally to exchange a word, wandering inexplicably in and out of the large shed that housed the equipment. No one paid him any attention. He appeared to have been forgotten.

He sat there in the heat and his eyelids became weighted. Soon enough he watched the yard through the thicket of his lashes. He tried to keep his eyes focused on his father's figure, but it elongated, distorted. He felt his head slump once, twice.

He woke to the sound of laughter. He was on the ground at the foot of the

hull, crumple-curled like a baby, drool
trailing from one side of his mouth. His
father and the others working the yard
were standing over him – one of the men
crying with mirth, his face creased up.

His father had stepped forward and
pulled him to his feet. 'You'd better stick
with me,' he said.

The boats that he took on did not
belong to rich men, but to working men
like himself. The way he worked was in-
stinctive. He approached each craft with
respect. He had an understanding and a
love of the jigsaw of pieces that made them
up, the texture and history of the wood.
'What can we do to get you shipshape?'
he would ask under his breath as he paced
around a boat, assessing it for himself,
regardless of what he had been told. He
didn't waste time when he got to work.

Pyotr stood all day watching his
father. At dusk they walked home. He fell
into bed, turned his face to the wall, slept.

When he was asked the next day if he would be coming to the yard he surprised himself by saying yes. By the end of the week he was pleased with the welts and scars that were collecting on his skin. His hands had blistered. His arms had developed muscles he had not known existed as he stripped and varnished the boats.

'What are we going to do when we reach the other side?' Golom asks. He is keeping up, but stops every few paces to take one step back before carrying on.

'Do you have to do that?'

'What?' Golom asks, this time taking two steps back.

'What makes you think we'll reach the other side?' Pyotr says. 'I'll have dealt with you long before then.'

'*Jay-sus!*' Golom darts ahead. 'You'll have to catch me.' He stops briefly, waits until Pyotr has nearly caught up with him, and then shoots off again. He is laughing a wheezy kind of laugh. He thinks he's funny. He keeps it going a good while – picking up speed by skidding in short bursts.

Pyotr has no plan for the other side except to catch a lift. If they are lucky with their timing they can try to hitch the school bus that runs the western stretch. That would take them a good way. They would be in before dark.

He is warm inside his cocoon of clothes. His legs are getting used to the rhythm. He pictures the school room – Limpet, chalk in hand; his classmates casting wondering glances towards his empty chair. He breathes in deeply and puffs out white flurries, imagining that it is smoke from a cigar, or cigarette.

He didn't think Limpet would bother to call his father.

*

There is a fissure an inch, two inches wide, tracing a path across the ice ahead of them. They stand looking down at it.

'It's nothing,' Pyotr says. 'It's just a crack.'

They take a step closer.

'There's no melt water,' he says.

Golom squats on the ice and lowers his hand into the crevice, pulls it out quickly, and lowers it again. He looks up at Pyotr, squinting in the sunlight, and releases a chuckle, something like a growl, from deep down in his throat.

'Come on,' Pyotr says.

The sun is much higher in the sky now.

They follow the same path as the crevice, pausing to inspect it now and then where it widens, and then carrying on. It meanders a little, but not much. It seems to be heading the way they want to go. They walk side by side, either side of it, keeping the far reaches of the lake on their right.

The way the crevice is etched in the ice reminds him of the fracture that still runs the length of their bedroom wall.

He remembers waking from his sleep to what he believed was a train going past, heavy with freight. His bed was vibrating. He had reached out and put one hand against the wall and found that it was pulsing too. And then he had heard the urgency in his father's voice. They had stood in the doorway. The next day they saw the fracture in the wall, and downstairs, plaster littering the floor like dirty snowfall.

Dec-Lan knew about fault lines, and tectonic plates, and volcanoes.

He was a geologist, with a sideline in marine biology – that was what he had said. He had swum deep down in the ocean near Iceland, and waited, and listened, and heard the sound of the earth pulling itself apart.

In the autumn, on the map on the school wall, Pyotr had found Iceland. He had put his finger on top of it, pressed down hard. He remembers Dec-Lan walking along the shore with the wetsuit pulled to his waist. He remembers the plastic shoes that he wore in the water, and that squelched when he walked.

'I am a geologist, with a sideline in marine biology,' Pyotr says, under his breath, as he walks. Dec-Lan had said that one day their lake would become an ocean, with the movement of the plates, the shifting of the earth.

'If we're going to do this hike across your lake,' he had said with a wink, 'we'd better do it soon.'

Pyotr stops and takes in the ice all around them, the distance they have to go until they reach the shore.

He imagines the vibration building, travelling through his body, making its way from his feet, through his calves, up his legs.

It would be slow at first – tiny fractures in the ice, barely visible, pencil marks scored across the lake. The sound would be glass shattering; a million splinters.

A sudden force and his vision blurs – his head thrown side to side, backwards and forwards. He sucks in great raw breaths of air. He is staggering, reeling, feet spread-eagled. When the ice ruptures, the noise is deafening. It is the sound of cities collapsing. The lake breaks into craggy, bobbing chunks. There is a final, fatal, immersion in the water.

Pyotr finds the lake still solid beneath their feet; but the air is changing. It becomes filmy, taking new form, cascading in gossamer curtains that filter the sunlight, sending it shafting in every direction at once. The sky vanishes. They are drenched in light and water – suspended with no above and no below. And then the mist thickens to a whiteout. Pyotr can't see his hands as he holds them to his face and when he looks down his feet have gone.

'Where are you?' he says.

No response.

'Hey. Where are you?'

'I'm right here. *Jay-sus*,' Golom says, close by.

'Well, don't wander off. Stay put.'

They stand there in silence for a moment. It is incredibly quiet. Pyotr can feel a fine cold spray falling on his skin. He hears Golom sigh and wonders how long it is going to last. His eyes are open, looking up and around to see what he can see, but there is nothing.

'I can see a face,' Golom says.

'No you can't.'

'I can see a face.'

'Don't be stupid.' He tries not to think about the lake spirits.

He tries not to think about the fissure.

Golom starts humming tunelessly, loudly. Pyotr knows that he's doing it to be annoying and is about to tell him to shut up, but finds that he likes it. He doesn't say a word. He stands in the middle of the whiteout smiling.

Dec-Lan's smiles would come and go easily and he was not used to this, did not know how to respond. Instead of just smiling back he would find himself staring. Dec-Lan would laugh – not unkindly – but he would laugh at him.

The mist lifts abruptly and space opens out just as quickly as it had disappeared.

The sun is bright in the sky. The air feels fresh. They walk on.

*

Later in the summer Dec-Lan's team had arrived with its own boat, and Pyotr would see them heading out much further than they had been in his father's small craft. There they would use sonar, and specialist diving equipment, and they would do tests underwater. He was told this at school, when the whole class was told about it in the autumn – the group of scientists who had come to study their lake, and who were now long gone.

Pyotr had watched the boat head out early in the morning from the other side, where they had set up their base. It followed the same route each time up the far shore. He had imagined Dec-Lan standing on the deck of the boat looking out. Pyotr would wave. He couldn't see anyone waving back, but doing it made him still feel connected to the man.

Dec-Lan had told them their lake was fifty million years old, four hundred miles long. He had told them that most of the species in the lake could only be found in this one lake in the whole world. He had told them that the geology of the area – the volcanoes, the earthquakes – was phenomenal. He had told them that the weather systems blew his mind – those storms, he said, that came in out of nowhere; those hurricanes; those monumental waves. 'I want to see that for myself,' he had said. 'I have to see that.'

At their feet the fissure has widened into something more impressive: a hole. It isn't a fishing hole. It's natural. The sides are smooth – polished even – vivid in the light. It is whorled like a shell, and changes colour gradually from white to sky-blue as it descends. It darkens finally into something deeper – like someone poured ink down there.

They lie, flat on their bellies, looking in. It's like peering down a well. They can hear water at the bottom – gurgling and sloshing about.

'Haalllooo!' Pyotr calls.

'Haalllooo!' It calls back.

'Ooooolla!' Golom yells.

'Ooooolla!' It yells back.

Golom rolls over, victorious, and lets out a cry. It takes flight.

Pyotr pulls the flask and the remainders of their lunch from the backpack. They eat, cross-legged, smiling like guardians at the mouth of it, before moving on.

'When we get to the other side,' Pyotr says, 'I reckon we can catch the bus.'

He thinks they're making good time. They are moving faster now, eager for the other side. The air feels charged, somehow alive.

'Imagine their faces,' Golom says.

Pyotr glances at his brother. 'I reckon we should play it down.'

Golom doesn't look convinced.

'If we get back early enough, we could just not tell,' Pyotr says.

'Dad?'

'Right.'

'Why?'

'So someone else would. It'd be better that way. He'd be really impressed because we hadn't even mentioned it ourselves.'

Golom's mouth falls open. He looks stunned. 'I'm telling him,' he says.

'That's fine.'

'I'm telling him.'

'If that's what you want.'

'I am.'

'That's OK,' Pyotr says. 'You're too young to understand.'

Golom hits him side on, knocking him back down onto the ice. He's all fists and rage. Though Pyotr tries to push him off he can't and soon he gives up and just takes the pelting.

'Take it back!' Golom shrieks, high-pitched.

'No.'

'Take it back!'

'Why would I take it back?' He's laughing but the fist-fall is starting to hurt. 'OK. Stop it.' He tries once more to shake Golom off.

'Take it back!'

'OK. I take it back. I take it back.'

They lie flat out on the ice catching their breath. Though the sun is still bright the blue has faded.

Pyotr cranes his head and looks at things upside down. He sees the paper mill, inverted, the building like a large pale bug, its legs in the air, the stilt-like props reaching up towards the earth.

'Train!' Golom yells.

All their lives they had heard the

sound of it, and if they were quick
enough caught sight of it too, steam
streaming behind, faces pressed to the
windows. It went to Vladivostock, to the
ocean. They had to imagine what that
was like – water to the other side of the
world.

'We should probably get up,' Pyotr
says, making no attempt to move. He
looks along the shoreline for their home.
He sees brittle trees lined up like ghost
people, mountains behind.

Dec-Lan had arrived on the train. He
had come with his talk of lichen and
gastropods and crustaceans. He had told
them he never wanted to go, never wanted
to leave these shores, these forests, these
mountains.

The colour of the shore has changed – a
deep, bruised blue underscores the
mountainside ahead. Pyotr looks at his
brother. 'Let's go,' he says. 'Not far

now.' He gets to his feet and pulls up his scarf. Golom fixes his balaclava so it covers his nose, but then yanks it back down. He is smiling. 'I can carry the bag now,' he says. 'You said.' As soon as he has the backpack they get going. The disc of the sun is now faint in the sky, glowing white on white behind gathering clouds.

Pyotr has known moments when the air and the land have taken on the look of an old photograph – everything washed with a kind of gold-brown, every detail picked out. This is happening now. Every tree trunk, every leafless branch, every roof, the sliver of the road running parallel to the shore – which is close now – the layered foothills, the mountains behind. Everything is carefully drawn.

'Look,' he says.

'What?'

'Do you see that?' he says. He pulls

down his scarf, stops to take it all in. He turns very slowly on the spot. 'You see that?' he shouts out, punching at the air with his fist.

Golom is pointing to the shore ahead of them. The ice has turned a muddy kind of black where it meets the beach.

Hail – suddenly – stinging the skin. It comes in horizontally.

'Cover up,' Pyotr says. 'Shit.'

Golom is looking at him and his mouth is open but no words are coming out, or if there are words they are being taken by the wind which is starting to howl at them like something malevolent come to life. Icy water is streaming down his face.

'Cover up,' Pyotr calls into the wind. 'Cover your face!'

His brother is immobile. His eyes are wide and scared.

'Hold onto me,' Pyotr shouts into his

ear. 'Hold on. OK?' He tries to tug the balaclava over his brother's face as he pulls him in.

The wind whips at them, buffeting. And snow now. A blinding white mass.

Pyotr's legs are knocked sideways as the full force hits them, his feet threatening to slip from under him. Keep steady, he tells himself. Hold on.

As close as he is to his brother he can no longer make out the features of his face. 'Stubby?' he yells. But it is point-less. There is no way of speaking or hearing in this. The wind cuts through to his skin, which is prickling, startled. His fingers are burning.

Closing his eyes against the squall he thinks how if he'd asked his father before heading off he would have known the answers to any question of distance, or orientation, or the time it would take them to cross the lake if they walked at a particular speed.

He pictures his father. And then he tries to picture his mother too. She's strange and serious. Like the photograph. He tries to remember her voice instead – the warmth of it – but what he hears is the wind.

The sound that makes it through his layers reminds him of the time he had water trapped in his ears after swimming, the feeling of being still submerged, the true sound of the world gone, speech lost, his own voice distorted even to himself, the noises inside his body magnified, the sounds outside that were normally so clear changed into something else, something rushing and creaking and complaining, like a haunted house.

Now he is with Dec-Lan suspended underwater, listening for the sound of the plates. His feet are moving slowly to keep himself in place. His arms are spread wide like an eagle, and he is smiling.

'Wake up,' he tells himself somewhere deep down. 'Swim.'

He cannot feel his arms holding his brother. His lashes are thick with snow now and he blinks to see, to reassure himself that he still has him. He's there – he sees his red balaclava – although he doesn't trust himself, doesn't trust his hands to hold on. He bends his knees and manoeuvres himself down onto the ice, brings Golom with him, covers his body with his own, tries to shield him from the wind and the snow.

Hovering in his mind, delicate, alive: his brother's wide eyes – irises like crystals, white-blue, pale and splintered.

'*You're-all-right,*' he murmurs to him now.

Improper Stories by Saki

A Favourite of the Gods
  by Sybille Bedford

A Compass Error
  by Sybille Bedford

Mendelssohn is on the Roof
  by Jiří Weil

Life with a Star by Jiří Weil

American Drolleries by Mark Twain

Kalimantaan by C. S. Godshalk

Illyrian Spring by Ann Bridge

Calm at Sunset, Calm at Dawn
  by Paul Watkins

The Architects by Stefan Heym

A Dance of Folly and Pleasure
  by O. Henry

DAUNT BOOKS CAN BE FOUND AT:

83 Marylebone High Street
London W1U 4QW
United Kingdom
Telephone: 020 7224 2295
Email: orders@dauntbooks.co.uk

158–164 Fulham Road
London SW10 9PR
United Kingdom
Telephone: 020 7373 4997
Email: chelsea@dauntbooks.co.uk

112–114 Holland Park Avenue
London W11 4UA
United Kingdom
Telephone: 020 7727 7022
Email: hollandpark@dauntbooks.co.uk

51 South End Road
London NW3 2QB
United Kingdom
Telephone: 020 7794 8206
Email: hampstead@dauntbooks.co.uk

193 Haverstock Hill
London NW3 4QL
United Kingdom
Telephone: 020 7794 4006
Email: belsizepark@dauntbooks.co.uk

61 Cheapside
London EC2V 6AX
United Kingdom
Telephone: 020 7248 1117
Email: cheapside@dauntbooks.co.uk

K. J. Orr would like to thank the
Arts and Humanities Research
Council for their support.

Arts & Humanities
Research Council